Barney Saltzberg

Dog

and Rabbit

Charlesbridge

For Andrea Wolman,
my lifelong friend

Published by Charlesbridge, 85 Main Street, Watertown, MA 02472 (617) 926-0329
www.charlesbridge.com

Library of Congress Cataloging-in-Publication Data
Names: Saltzberg, Barney, author, illustrator.
Title: Dog and Rabbit / Barney Saltzberg.
Description: Watertown, MA : Charlesbridge, [2019] | Summary: "Dog and Rabbit are both a little lonely
    and in search of a friend, but Rabbit is initially too distracted by the bunny he sees through the window
    to notice that Dog is just the friend that he has been looking for"—Provided by publisher.
Identifiers: LCCN 2018035163 (print) | LCCN 2018041704 (ebook) | ISBN 9781632898661 (ebook) | ISBN
    9781632898678 (ebook pdf) | ISBN 9781623541071 (reinforced for library use)
Subjects: LCSH: Dogs—Juvenile fiction. | Rabbits—Juvenile fiction. | Friendship—Juvenile fiction.
    | Loneliness—Juvenile fiction. | CYAC: Dogs—Fiction. | Rabbits—Fiction. | Friendship—Fiction.
    | Loneliness—Fiction. | LCGFT: Picture books.
Classification: LCC PZ7.S1552 (ebook) | LCC PZ7.S1552 Do 2019 (print) | DDC [E]—dc23
LC record available at https://lccn.loc.gov/2018035163

Printed in China
(hc) 10 9 8 7 6 5 4 3 2 1

Illustrations made using Kyle Brushes in Photoshop, drawn on a Wacom Cintiq
Display set in Changing by PintassilgoPrints, text type set in Rabbits Bro by Piñata
Color separations by Colourscan Print Co Pte Ltd, Singapore
Printed by 1010 Printing International Limited in Huizhou, Guangdong, China
Production supervision by Brian G. Walker
Designed by Susan Mallory Sherman

DOG

Dog was fine being alone.

But sometimes Dog was lonely.

Dog wanted a friend.

Someone to play with.

Someone to walk with.

Someone to be with.

"How hard can it be to find a friend?" he wondered.

It was harder than he thought.

It would take time.

Rabbit

Rabbit was fine being alone.

But sometimes Rabbit was lonely.

Rabbit wanted a friend.

Someone to play with.

Someone to hop with.

Someone to be with.

"How hard can it be to find a friend?" he wondered.

It was harder than he thought.

It would take time.

Dog saw Rabbit looking in the window of his house.

Rabbit thought the bunny
would be a nice friend.

Rabbit smiled at the bunny.

Dog smiled at Rabbit.

And Rabbit hopped away.

This went on for days.
Dog waited for Rabbit.

Rabbit arrived.
Rabbit smiled at the bunny.

Dog smiled at Rabbit.

And Rabbit hopped away.

Dog often thought
about Rabbit.

Rabbit often thought
about the bunny.

One morning the door was open.

Rabbit saw that the bunny was not real!

The bunny was not waiting for him after all.

The one who had waited . . .

Now, Dog still waits for Rabbit.

Dog smiles.

. . . smiles back.